Mini Submarine

12 Ballgowns

3 Puppies
Lots of new tiaras!
A talking PARROT ✓

Squirrel!

JEWELRY!

HUMUNGOUS cake !!

A BIG Tv ✓

Cell phone

My own helicopter.   Teddy Bears ✓

Cuddly bunnies ✓

books ✓   ROCKET?

Puzzles ✓

MOVIES

Ruby

The Princess and the Presents

For Mum
C. H.

For Lee, just for everything
S. W.

First U.S. edition 2014

Library of Congress Catalog Card Number 2013955660
ISBN 978-0-7636-7398-7

14 15 16 17 18 19 FGF 10 9 8 7 6 5 4 3 2 1

Printed in Shenzhen, Guangdong, China

This book was typeset in ThrohandInk.
The illustrations were done in mixed media.

Nosy Crow
An imprint of
Candlewick Press
99 Dover Street
Somerville, Massachusetts 02144

www.nosycrow.com
www.candlewick.com

The Princess and the Presents

Carys Hart

Sarah Warburton

I ♥ Presents

nosy crow

An imprint of Candlewick Press

"It's Princess Ruby's birthday soon!"
the king cried in a tizzy.
The maids were all in such a whirl,
it made the footmen dizzy.

The people all across the land
were making preparations,
baking cakes and fine desserts
for the coming celebrations.

High up in her tower,
little Ruby lounged in bed.
"My special day must be the best—
or else!" the princess said.

She shouted out her orders
while the servants bowed and smiled.

She yelled and bawled
and stomped her feet.
She was a horrid child.

"I want a giant tree house and a parrot that can talk.

Bye!

I want a pair of fancy shoes that light up when I walk.

Monday

Tuesday

Wednesday

Thursday

Friday

I need a new tiara to wear each day at school.

And a pony and some roller skates
and lots and lots of jewels.

I want a massive birthday feast
with cupcakes and ice cream.

If not, I'll lie down on the floor
and scream and scream and . . .

SCREAM!"

"Of course, my darling," soothed the king,
and down the stairs he dashed.
He rushed out to the grandest stores
with a suitcase full of cash.

RICHY RICH & CO

He chose the very nicest things
that royal coins could get,
to ensure that Ruby's special day
would be the best one yet.

Soon the big day was upon them,
and the king was full of cheer,

"I WANT MY PRESENTS!"
Ruby yelled, and shoved her dad aside.

so he went to wake his daughter

with a "HAPPY BIRTHDAY, dear!"

She ran down to the ballroom,
and this is what she spied. . . .

She grabbed the biggest gift of all.
She didn't even smile.
She ripped the pretty paper off
and tossed it in a pile.

"But where's my giant tree house?"
bawled the greedy little tyke.
"You promised me a cell phone,
three puppies, *and* a bike!"

"There, there, my dear," replied the king
as he opened up the door.

The servants brought more boxes in
and heaped them on the floor.

They piled up all the presents
on the tables and the chairs.

They built them into towers
all along the palace stairs.

They filled up all the bedrooms
and the bathrooms and the halls.

There were presents in the kitchen
and stacked up against the walls.

"That's more like it!" Ruby shouted.
"It's just what I deserve.
I'll open all my presents,
then my banquet can be served."

But . . .

as she spoke, there came a creak. The ceiling bowed and groaned.
The walls began to crack. "What *now*?" the princess moaned.
"The palace is collapsing!" the worried king replied.
"Too many gifts! Now, Ruby, dear,
you've got to get outside!"

"Make sure to save my brand-new stuff!" the selfish princess whined.
"Every box and package—
don't leave anything behind!"
The brave king raced along the hall, dodging falling plaster.
Then with a crash, the roof caved in—

a terrible disaster!

"What *have* I done?" wailed Ruby.
"The best gift I ever had
is buried in a pile of bricks.
PLEASE! Help me save . . .

my DAD!

There's no present as important as the person I adore.
I'd give up all my birthday gifts to see my dad once more."

The firefighters spread the word:
"His Highness is in trouble!"
Kind people came from far and wide
To search beneath the rubble.

After hours and hours of digging,
they heard some quiet knocks . . .

sniff
sniff

and found His Royal Highness safe
inside a cardboard box!

"My darling little Ruby,
  I'm so sorry," sighed the king.
"Your birthday's wrecked. Your home is gone.
  I've ruined everything."

"But, Daddy," Ruby shouted,
"all I really want is you!
I see that I've been selfish,
and I know just what to do.

We'll build the little tree house,
and we'll line the floor with rugs.
This piece of cake is still OK,
and, look, I've found some mugs."

sniff
sniff

Then she made the helpful people
a nice hot pot of tea . . .

and lived happily ever after
with her daddy in a tree.